OLIVER TWIST
by Charles Dickens
Retold as a play by Keith West

Illustrations by George Cruikshank,
taken from the original,
serialised version of *Oliver Twist*, 1837

About this play

This play is a dramatised version of the novel *Oliver Twist* by Charles Dickens, which was first published in serial form, in 1837. The illustrations used in this play are taken from the original novel.

Charles Dickens (1812 – 1870) is regarded as one of the greatest novelists of his time. Many people think he is the finest English writer after Shakespeare.

Dickens created many memorable and colourful characters but he also made people think. Dickens was a revolutionary writer, he wanted things to change. He spent much of his life fighting tyranny and injustice – and this comes through strongly in the novel *Oliver Twist.* He wrote so that the Victorian public would be aware of the reality of life in parts of London.

Dickens wrote about the London of the 1820s, which was the scene of some of his childhood and early adulthood. During this time, London became the largest city in Europe. The population expanded and people came from the rural countryside and from Ireland in search of work.

In the London of the 1820s, the poor stayed together in large numbers in what were known as 'Rookeries'. Like rooks, the poor just about made a living, amid much vice and squalor. Oliver Twist's London was a rotting, reeking, rabbit-warren of alleyways where ragged children played barefoot in mud and slime. There were drunks and criminals at almost every turn. Gangs hid in the rookeries – gangs like the one Fagin runs in *Oliver Twist* were a reality.

Oliver Twist is a great novel and Dickens was only in his mid-twenties when he wrote the story. The novel depicts life in the poorhouse – a public institution that housed the poor – and follows Oliver's fortunes and misfortunes until justice is done to the boy.

I hope that this adaptation will encourage a new generation to read Dickens' great novel.

Keith West 2000

CHARACTERS

Narrator	
Oliver Twist	a poor orphan boy
Mother	Oliver's young mother, who dies
Sally	an old worker at the poorhouse
Surgeon	doctor who delivered Oliver
Mr Bumble	parish beadle
Mr Monks	a mysterious character, who wants Oliver dead
1st Gentleman }	two of the board
2nd Gentleman }	
Henry　　　　 }	two boys at the poorhouse
Ben　　　　　}	
Cook	worker at the poorhouse
Mr Gamfield	chimney sweep
Mr Sowerberry	undertaker
Mrs Sowerberry	undertaker's wife
Noah Claypole	works for Mr Sowerberry
Charlotte	maid to the Sowerberrys
Mr Bayton	man whose wife has just died
Old Woman	mother of Mrs Bayton
Jack Dawkins	known as the Artful Dodger
Boy	works for Fagin
Fagin	an old thief
Mr Brownlow	a kind old man
Policeman	
Mr Fang	police magistrate
Mr Grimwig	friend of Mr Brownlow
Bill Sikes	a thief
1st Bystander	
2nd Bystander	
Brittles　　　 }	servants of Mrs Maylie
Giles　　　　　}	
Mrs Maylie	upper class old lady

For my brother, Brian … who shared my childhood

3

OLIVER TWIST

ACT ONE SCENE ONE

At the poorhouse

NARRATOR: A lady struggles to arrive at the poorhouse. She is heavily pregnant and in pain. Mr Bumble allows her to enter and she falls to the ground. A surgeon is called.

SURGEON: I suppose this young slip of a girl has no husband?

SALLY: *(Sipping gin from a bottle)* Lor' no. What do you expect, eh? *(She laughs)*

SURGEON: Come on, give me a hand. She's about to deliver.

SALLY: *(Sipping gin)* It ain't my job to help. I'll sit close by the fire and drink. The night's a cold one.

NARRATOR: The surgeon delivers the baby.

SURGEON: Why, it's a boy. But the poor little thing won't breathe. *(Alarmed)* It's as if the baby does not want to be part of this world.

SALLY: *(Struggling up from her chair)* Doctors; no damn good. *(She grabs hold of the baby and slaps him hard. The baby cries.)* See, it's alive all right.

MOTHER: Let me see my baby, my child. Let me hold my boy before I die.

SURGEON: Oh, you must not talk about dying yet. *(Softly)* You are so young and you have a child to look after.

SALLY: Lor' bless her heart, no. Think what it is to be a mother.

MOTHER: *(Tearful)* But my heart's broken.

SALLY: I can tell you - when you've had thirteen children, all dead but two...

SURGEON: The young lady. She's dead. *(Checks her pulse and looks down at her hands)* The same old story – no wedding ring. *(Picks up his hat)* Good night! *(He walks briskly away)*

SALLY: *(To herself)* Let's see if the young lady is worth anything. Some are, some ain't. Ah, a gold brooch! Ha ha! *(She takes the brooch)* That'll be worth a bob or two. It'll keep me in gin ....Or maybe I'll keep a hold of it!

(Mr Bumble enters)

Mr BUMBLE: What's the fuss?

SALLY: *(Hiding the brooch)* Woman dead, boy born, 'tis all!

Mr BUMBLE: Boy born? What's the mother called?

SALLY: *(Sits on her chair near the fire)* Don't know, sir.

Mr BUMBLE: *(Looking at the dead body)* Sad, very sad. She had a pretty face. *(Turns to the baby)* He's crying heartily enough. Bet he'll be trouble for us all, eh Sally? What'll we call the young sprat? *(thinks)* Down to 'T'. Twist – Oliver Twist. That's what we'll call him. Oliver Twist! Next one will be a 'U'. Goodnight Sally.

SALLY: Goodnight Mr Bumble. *(To herself)* The brooch will keep me in gin. Must get home now. Someone else can look after the baby. *(Walks towards the gates)* Done my bit for the night.

Mr MONKS:	*(Hurried)* Ah, excuse me.
SALLY:	*(Fearful, as Monks is ugly and his pale face is frightening)* Yes?
Mr MONKS:	Has a young woman, a woman expecting a child, been brought in?
SALLY:	*(Fingering the gold brooch)* No.
Mr MONKS:	Are you sure?
SALLY:	*(Hiding the brooch behind her back)* I would be the one to know, sir. I ain't seen no young pregnant woman here for over a year.
Mr MONKS:	Damn! If you do see a young pregnant woman, ask for me at the bank down the road. Monks is the name. Ask for Mr Monks. Got that?
SALLY:	Mr Monks… yes. I won't forget. *(Mr Monks runs off)* Ah, little Oliver Twist, I'll keep my eye on you. *(To the retreating Monks)* You'd 'ave wanted the brooch *(Looks at it)* and I'd reckon it's worth a bob or two!

SCENE TWO

NARRATOR:	The baby is now aged nine. He has been brought up by the Parish, and is a weak, pale, thin boy – thanks to workhouse meals.
Mr BUMBLE:	I am the parish beadle. That means I am in charge of you, young Oliver Twist. Now I don't want you to make trouble for me.
OLIVER:	No, sir.

Mr BUMBLE:	*(Irritated)* So, come along and meet the board. They have the money to buy your food, to keep you alive. They have the power to throw you out on the streets and let you starve. Understand?
OLIVER:	Yes, sir.
	(Mr Bumble leads Oliver into a room where eight fat gentlemen sit. They are eating and drinking. Oliver is very frightened.)
Mr BUMBLE:	Bow to the board, Oliver.
	(Oliver bows to the gentlemen around the table)
1st GENTLEMAN:	What's your name, boy?
OLIVER:	*(Very quietly)* Oliver Twist, sir.
1st GENTLEMAN:	Boy, you know you're an orphan, I suppose?
OLIVER:	What's that, sir?
1st GENTLEMAN:	*(Loud)* The boy's a fool!
2nd GENTLEMAN:	*(Kindly)* You know you haven't a father or mother?
OLIVER:	*(Very quietly)* Yes, sir.
2nd GENTLEMAN:	Well, now you know you are an orphan.
1st GENTLEMAN:	*(Loud)* After living here at our expense, you will be taught a useful trade and you will make something of your life. Now go, boy!
	(Oliver leaves the room with Mr Bumble. He is put in a room with other parish boys. They are working on various tasks.)

HENRY:	*(Angry)* We don't get enough food in this place. We're all starving. Before my dad died, I ate meat for every meal.
BEN:	We have to make do with what we're given.
HENRY:	*(Really angry)* Don't give me that! I tell you, if I'm not given more meat, I'll eat one of you.
OLIVER:	*(Frightened)* What shall we do?
BEN:	We'll draw lots. Whoever gets the shortest straw, will ask the cook for more food.
OLIVER:	We can't do that!
HENRY:	*(Brightens up)* We can and we will – or, I'll eat one of you.
	(They draw lots. Henry holds the straws, winks at the others and makes sure Oliver loses. That evening, after eating their gruel, the boys nudge Oliver.)
HENRY:	Go on then – what are you waiting for?
BEN:	You can't let us down.
	(Oliver rises from the table and walks over to the cook. He holds his basin and spoon in his hands.)
OLIVER:	*(Quietly)* Please sir, I want some more.
COOK:	What!
OLIVER:	*(Louder)* Please sir, I want some more.
COOK:	*(Trying to hit Oliver with a ladle)* Mr Bumble, Mr Bumble, here please. Rebellion!
Mr BUMBLE:	*(Emerging from another room)* What is the matter, cook?

COOK:	*(Points at Oliver)* This boy has asked for more.
Mr BUMBLE:	What? Asked for more? This cannot be!
1st GENTLEMAN:	*(Entering the room)* That boy will be hung. I know that boy will be hung.
2nd GENTLEMAN:	No, no, not yet. We'll sell him for five pounds. That way, the parish gains money.
1st GENTLEMAN:	I was never so convinced of anything in my life: I am sure the boy *(points at Oliver)* will come to be hanged.

SCENE THREE

Mr Gamfield, a chimney sweep, reads the notice that offers Oliver Twist for sale.

Mr GAMFIELD: *(to himself)* Five pounds? That will do fine. The last two boys died, stuck up chimneys. I hope this one will be thinner and then he might last a little longer.

(he notices the 1st Gentleman)

Ha! I wants to 'prentis a boy in the chimbley sweepin' business.

1st GENTLEMAN: Walk in to my office. *(Smiles)* We have a boy for you.

2nd GENTLEMAN: A nasty trade, chimney sweeping. Young boys have been smothered in chimneys before now.

Mr GAMFIELD: *(Scratches his head)* That's 'cause they get the smoke. Smoke ain't o' no use at all in making a boy come down. It sinds him to sleep. Boys is wery obstinit and wery lazy. A good, hot blaze makes 'em come down quick enough.

2nd GENTLEMAN: We the board do not approve of your proposition, Mr Gamfield.

1st GENTLEMAN: But....

(Mr Bumble enters, having overheard some of the conversation.)

Mr BUMBLE: You can't have Oliver Twist, sir. Not for that price.

1st GENTLEMAN: Offer us less. We'll let him go for four pounds. *(Laughs)* Yes four pounds, as long as you beat him now and again. Bumble, go fetch the boy!

(Mr Bumble brings Oliver before the board and Gamfield.)

Mr BUMBLE: Here is the boy.

Mr GAMFIELD: I hope you like chimbley-sweepin'!

OLIVER: *(Remains silent until pinched by Mr Bumble)* Yes, sir.

Mr GAMFIELD: *(With an ugly leer)* When I says I'll look after him, I means I will.

OLIVER: *(To Mr Bumble, tearful)* Starve me, beat me, kill me – but don't send me away with that dreadful man.

Mr BUMBLE: *(Aims a blow at Oliver)* Of all the artful and designing orphans that ever I see, Oliver, you are the most bare-faced that…

2nd GENTLEMAN: *(Interrupting)* Be quiet, Mr Bumble! I will not let the boy go.

1st GENTLEMAN: But…

2nd GENTLEMAN: *(Interrupting)* We'll send the boy back to the workhouse. He needs kind treatment. Look at the boy – he's a nervous wreck!

1st GENTLEMAN: That boy will be hanged. I'm sure of it!

Mr BUMBLE: Certainly!

2nd GENTLEMAN: Maybe – but the chimney-sweeping trade is a cruel one. The boy would have met certain death.

Mr GAMFIELD: Have you any other boys?

2nd GENTLEMAN: Certainly not, Mr Gamfield. Goodbye!

(Mr Gamfield walks out. At the door is an undertaker called Sowerberry. He enters as the two gentlemen and Oliver leave the room.)

Mr BUMBLE:	You've come to measure up for coffins?
Mr SOWERBERRY:	Indeed.
Mr BUMBLE:	You'll make your fortune, the rate children die here, Mr Sowerberry.
Mr SOWERBERRY:	Yes, but the money I receive here is so small.
Mr BUMBLE:	*(laughs)* Ah, but so are the coffins, Mr Sowerberry.
Mr SOWERBERRY:	Since the new feeding system was introduced, the coffins have become somewhat narrower and more shallow.
Mr BUMBLE:	*(Changing the subject)* Do you know anybody who wants a boy, as an apprentice? He's a millstone around our necks.
Mr SOWERBERRY:	I could do with a helper. Yes, I'll take the boy myself – he can help me make the coffins.
Mr BUMBLE:	*(Hurried)* I'll fetch the boy – see if you approve!
Mr SOWERBERRY:	Bring him round to my house, Mr Bumble. We'll see what Mrs Sowerberry thinks of the boy.
	(Later, at the undertaker's house)
Mr BUMBLE:	*(Shouting through the door)* I've brought the boy, Mr Sowerberry.
Mr SOWERBERRY:	Aha! *(Looking at Oliver)* Oh, that's the boy is it?

Mrs SOWERBERRY: Dear me, he's very small.

Mr BUMBLE: He is small, there's no denying it, ma'am. But he will grow, he'll grow.

Mrs SOWERBERRY: *(Nasty)* I dare say he will grow, on our food and drink. Parish children always cost more to keep than they're worth. However, *(glaring at Mr Sowerberry)* men always think they know best. *(To Oliver)* Get down stairs, little bag o' bones. *(Shouts)* Charlotte!

(A young serving maid appears)

Charlotte, take the bag o' bones downstairs and give him the food I'd put out for Trip. That dog hasn't come home since morning, so the boy can have the food. *(To Mr Bumble)* Trip always likes his food fresh.

CHARLOTTE: *(to Oliver)* Hope you like food prepared for dogs, boy!

OLIVER: If it's meat, I'll eat it!

Mrs SOWERBERRY: Boy, you'll have to sleep amongst the coffins. There's nowhere else to sleep so make the best of it! Hope you don't believe in ghosts and such.

(Charlotte dances away laughing)

SCENE FOUR

Oliver awakes the following morning. There is a loud noise, as if somebody is trying to kick down the door.

NOAH: *(A large vicious-looking boy, shouting through the door)* Open the door, will yer?

OLIVER: *(Polite)* I will directly, sir.

NOAH: I suppose you're the new boy, ain't yer?

OLIVER: Yes, sir.

NOAH: How old are yer?

OLIVER: Ten, sir.

NOAH: Then I'll whop yer when I get in, you see if I don't whop yer, work'us brat.

(Noah walks into the basement, where Oliver stands by the coffins.)

OLIVER: I beg your pardon. Did you knock?

NOAH: *(Taking a slice of bread from his pocket)* I kicked! Suppose, work'us, you don't know who I am?

(Oliver shakes his head)

I'm Mr Noah Claypole. You'll do as I say. *(Kicks Oliver's shin)* Take down the shutters and let's 'ave some light, you idle young ruffian.

(Charlotte enters. She winks at Noah)

CHARLOTTE: *(To Noah)* Come near the fire. I've saved some bacon for you from Master's breakfast *(To Oliver)* Open the shop, d' yer hear?

NOAH: *(Spitting out bacon fat)* D' ye hear, work'us?

CHARLOTTE:	What a rum creature you are, Noah. Why don't you leave the poor orphan alone?
NOAH:	*(Chokes on bacon)* Leave 'im alone? *(coughs)* His father and mother left 'im alone!
	(Noah and Charlotte laugh and walk out arm in arm.)
Mr SOWERBERRY:	*(Bursting into the room)* Hurry up, Oliver. Collect a black hat and follow me. We've a corpse to pick up.
	(Oliver shudders as Mr Sowerberry pushes him up the steps.)
	Hurry, Oliver, hurry.
NARRATOR:	An hour later, Mr Sowerberry and Oliver arrive at a large, dilapidated old house.
Mr BAYTON:	*(Shakes his fist at Mr Sowerberry)* Nobody shall go near her. Keep back, damn you. Keep back, or die.
Mr SOWERBERRY:	Nonsense, Mr Bayton.
Mr BAYTON:	She died in the dark, in the dark. I never knew *(sobbing)* I never knew how bad her fever was, until she died. *(Sobs)* I should have given her a candle, a light.
OLD WOMAN:	Lord, lord! How strange that I who gave birth to her should see her buried!
Mr SOWERBERRY:	*(To Mr Bayton)* Help me get Mrs Bayton into the coffin.
Mr BAYTON:	No, no. She was a good wife, a good wife.
	(They place the corpse into the coffin.)
Mr SOWERBERRY:	Pay your last respects, Mr Bayton. I shall collect the coffin tomorrow. Good day.

(Outside the house)

(Chuckles) Well, well. And how do you like the undertaking trade, Oliver?

OLIVER: *(Shivering)* Not very much, sir.

Mr SOWERBERRY: Ah, you'll get used to it in time, Oliver. This is a sickly season. You'll see plenty of bodies. You'll get used to bodies, coffins and mourners.

NARRATOR: A month later, Oliver and Noah are tidying the coffins.

NOAH: *(Vicious)* Work'us, I reckon old Sowerberry likes you better than me.

OLIVER: *(Careful)* I don't know about that, sir.

NOAH: *(Taunting)* Work'us, how's yer mother?

OLIVER: *(Hurt)* She's dead. Don't you say anything about her.

NOAH: *(Goading)* What did she die of, work'us?

OLIVER: *(Tearful)* She died of a broken heart. That's what old Sally told me. Don't you say anything bad about her. You'd better not.

NOAH: Better not? Why, your mother was a regular right-down bad'un. Good job she died when she did!

(Oliver, suddenly angry and upset, grabs Noah by the throat. He hits Noah hard. Noah falls down.)

OLIVER: *(Shouting)* Don't you say anything bad about my mother.

NOAH: *(A coward, Noah is quickly frightened)* Help! *(Shouts)* Work'us is murdering me!

CHARLOTTE: *(Rushes into the room)* Oh, oh, my poor Noah. *(She grabs hold of Oliver)* You little wretch.

Mrs SOWERBERRY: *(Staring at Oliver through the doorway)* What a mercy we haven't all been murdered in our beds.

CHARLOTTE: Mercy indeed! Poor Noah. He was all but killed!

Mrs SOWERBERRY: Mr Sowerberry is out on an errand, what shall we do? *(Thinks)* Ah yes. Noah, run and fetch Mr Bumble.

NARRATOR:	A short while later, Mr Bumble arrives at the house. Oliver is locked in the basement.
Mr BUMBLE:	*(Shouts through the keyhole)* Oliver, do you know this voice?
OLIVER:	*(Hiding under the coffins)* Yes.
Mr BUMBLE:	Ain't you afraid of it, young Twist?
OLIVER:	*(Boldly)* No!
	(A horrified gasp from Mrs Sowerberry, a groan from Charlotte.)
Mrs SOWERBERRY:	Mr Bumble, the boy must be mad.
Mr BUMBLE:	It's not madness, ma'am, it's meat. If you'd kept the boy on gruel, this would never have happened.
Mrs SOWERBERRY:	Dear, dear. I told Mr Sowerberry the same thing. We've been too liberal.
Mr BUMBLE:	His mother made her way to the poorhouse against difficulties and pain that would have killed most people. It's in the blood, ma'am. He comes from a bad line.
OLIVER:	*(Crying)* My mother was not bad!
	(Mr Sowerberry enters, dressed in funeral black)
Mr SOWERBERRY:	Now, what's all the fuss about, Oliver?
OLIVER:	Noah Claypole called my mother bad names.
Mrs SOWERBERRY:	Your mother deserved what Noah said, and more. You are an ungrateful little wretch.

OLIVER:	She didn't deserve to be called bad names! You're all liars!
	(Mrs Sowerberry bursts into tears. Charlotte groans louder. Noah hides a grin.)
Mr SOWERBERRY:	Sorry Oliver, I have no alternative but to beat you.

SCENE FIVE

NARRATOR:	The following morning, Oliver creeps out of Mr Sowerberry's house. He has decided to run away. He is walking towards central London when he is spotted by a small, thin boy of about thirteen.
JACK:	Hullo my covey, what's the row?
OLIVER:	I am hungry and tired and I've run away from a horrible place.
JACK:	Got any lodgings? Any money?
OLIVER:	*(Close to tears)* No.
JACK:	*(Whistles)* I'm Jack Dawkins. I know an old gentleman who'll put you up. People call me the Artful Dodger. Come on, follow me! *(Later)* We're almost at the old gentleman's house.
OLIVER:	*(Shocked)* But the house – it's falling down.
JACK:	*(Ignores Oliver and whistles three times)*
BOY:	Dodger!
JACK:	Is Fagin upstairs?
BOY:	He's sortin' through the wipes. Upstairs with you!

(Upstairs, the room is dirty and black. Oliver notices an old man, dressed in a drab flannel gown.)

George Cruikshank

JACK: *(To Oliver, but pointing out the old man)* This is Fagin. *(To Fagin)* This is my friend, Oliver Twist.

FAGIN:	We are very glad to see you, Oliver, very. *(To Jack)* Dodger, take off the sausages *(indicates a pan of sizzling sausages on an open-fire)*. Let young Oliver sit near the fire. *(Oliver sits by the fire, but stares at a long line of handkerchiefs)*. Ah, you notice the pocket handkerchiefs, my dear. We've got them ready for a wash. Ha, ha, ha! Oliver Twist, eh? Ha, ha, ha.
	(Oliver, tired out, falls asleep by the fire.)
	Oliver Twist eh? We'll teach the boy a thing or two, eh Dodger?
NARRATOR:	The following morning, Oliver wakes up to hear Fagin talking to himself. He is sorting through a box of jewels.
FAGIN:	What a fine thing capital punishment is! Dead men never repent, never bring awkward stories to light. Five of them strung up in a row, not one can grass on me. *(Fagin rubs his hands together)* Ha, ha.
	(Fagin notices Oliver is looking at him. Fagin takes a knife from his pocket and walks towards Oliver.)
	What do you watch me for? What have you heard me say? Speak out, boy or you die.
OLIVER:	*(Innocently)* Sorry sir, I woke up just now.
FAGIN:	*(Relaxing)* Did you see any *(Closes jewel box)* of the pretty things, my dear?
OLIVER:	*(Naïvely)* Yes, sir.

FAGIN:	Ah well, my dear, some people call me a miser.... but they're mine, the pretty things, all mine. They're all I have put away for my old age, Oliver.
	(Jack, the artful dodger, knocks and enters.)
FAGIN:	I hope you've been hard at work this morning, Dodger. What have you got?
JACK:	*(Proud)* A couple of pocket books... and some wipes.
FAGIN:	*(Rubbing his hands together)* Good, good, my dear. Ha, ha! *(He casts an eye over the stolen goods)* Well made, yes, very well made. We'll teach Oliver how to...er....make wipes.*(To Oliver)* Would you like that, my dear?
OLIVER:	*(Enthusiastically)* Oh yes please, sir.
FAGIN:	*(To Jack)* He's very green is this one.
JACK:	*(To Fagin)* He'll learn, given time.
NARRATOR:	Fagin, Jack and the boy turn pick-pocketing into a game. Oliver, after a while, becomes good at 'the game'.
FAGIN:	Splendid, Oliver, splendid. What a bright boy you are, my dear. *(To Jack)* Take him out, Dodger. He's ready.
NARRATOR:	In the London streets, Jack sees an old man near a bookstall. He is Mr Brownlow.
JACK:	*(Pointing)* Do you see the old cove by the bookstall?
OLIVER:	Yes, I do see him.
JACK:	*(Winks)* He'll do.

(Jack sneaks up to the old man and steals his handkerchief.)

OLIVER: *(Shocked)* So… it wasn't a game. Fagin and the gang are criminals. I can't stay here. I'll have to run away again.

(Oliver starts to run. Mr Brownlow finds his handkerchief missing.)

Mr BROWNLOW: *(Turns round and sees Oliver running away)* Stop thief!

JACK: *(Urgent)* Come on, Oliver. Run over here!

Mr BROWNLOW:	*(Shouts)* Stop, thief!
	(Oliver falls over an apple-cart in his haste to get away.)
POLICEMAN:	Is that the thief, sir?
	(The policeman points at Oliver, Mr Brownlow nods)
OLIVER:	*(To Mr Brownlow)* It wasn't me, I stole nothing. It was another boy.
POLICEMAN:	*(Looking down at Oliver)* Oh yes? Tell us another one.
Mr BROWNLOW:	Don't hurt the boy.
POLICEMAN:	*(Hauls Oliver to his feet)* Stand up, you young ruffian.

SCENE SIX

Oliver is brought before the police magistrate, Mr Fang. The old gentleman, Mr Brownlow, accompanies Oliver.

Mr BROWNLOW:	*(To Fang)* Could the boy be innocent? There is something in that face… something I have seen somewhere before. No, no. I cannot recall.
Mr FANG:	*(Looking up from his desk full of papers)* Who are you?
Mr BROWNLOW:	I am Mr Brownlow.
Mr FANG:	*(To police officer)* What's the fellow charged with?
POLICEMAN:	*(Trying not to laugh)* He's not charged at all. He appears against the boy, your worship.
Mr FANG:	What's the boy done?

POLICEMAN:	The boy looks ill.
Mr FANG:	Nonsense!

(Oliver faints and falls to the ground)

Mr BROWNLOW:	*(bending over Oliver)* Poor boy, poor boy. Fetch a coach, I'll not press charges.

(Jack, the Artful Dodger, peers through the window, listening. He then runs off to Fagin's house.)

FAGIN:	*(Sharp)* Where is Oliver?
JACK:	The traps have got him.
FAGIN:	Careless, careless boy.

(At that moment, Bill Sikes enters. He is a big lout of a man. Following him is a flea-ridden black and white dog.)

BILL:	*(To the dog)* Come on, d'ye hear. Fagin, what's the news? You look glum, old man.
FAGIN:	One of my new boys is captured. He may say something that could get us all into trouble.
BILL:	Give us some spirits!

(Fagin, afraid of Bill Sikes, offers him a tumbler of whisky.)

We must get a hold of the boy again.

(Nancy, Bill's girlfriend, enters. She is fair-haired and pale.)

You'll get a hold of the boy, won't you Nancy?

NANCY:	No, no.
BILL:	She'll go, Fagin.

NANCY:	No, she won't, Fagin.
BILL:	*(Threatening Nancy)* Yes she will, Fagin. She'll go, or she'll end up black and blue.
FAGIN:	*(To Nancy)* Pretend the boy Oliver is your young brother, my dear.
NANCY:	*(Acting)* Oh, my brother, my poor, dear, sweet innocent, my dear.
	(Nancy bursts into tears)
FAGIN:	*(Fagin rubs his hands together)* Very good, very good, my dear.
BILL:	She'll do. She's an honour to her sex. Here, Fagin, fill up my tumbler with spirits. Find out what's happened to the boy, Nancy.
NARRATOR:	Later, Nancy returns. Bill has drunk too much and is sleeping.
NANCY:	*(To Fagin)* An old gentleman took Oliver, a Mr Brownlow.
FAGIN:	We need to have the boy back. He may blab about us. We will have to stop his mouth, or we're done for.

ACT TWO SCENE ONE

NARRATOR:	Oliver is recovering from a fever. He is at Mr Brownlow's house. Mr Grimwig, a friend of Brownlow, is with them.
Mr BROWNLOW:	Oliver, I will allow you to read any book in my library. Do you like reading?
OLIVER:	*(Enthusiastic)* Oh, yes sir.
Mr BROWNLOW:	Good. The friends I held dearest are all in their graves. You are a friendless orphan. You shall never be friendless again, as long as I live.

Mr GRIMWIG:	*(Stern)* You cannot trust boys.
Mr BROWNLOW:	I can trust this one with my life.
Mr GRIMWIG:	Bah! He's an orphan. All boys brought up in the workhouse are scoundrels.
Mr BROWNLOW:	Mr Grim -
Mr GRIMWIG:	You've been hoodwinked, taken in, my friend.
Mr BROWNLOW:	*(Angry)* Then we shall test Oliver. *(Gathers up a pile of books from the table.)* Here Oliver, take these to the bookstall for me.
OLIVER:	*(Eager)* Certainly, sir. I shall be back in ten minutes, sir.
	(Oliver leaves with the books)
Mr GRIMWIG:	Now Brownlow, my old friend, you won't see that boy again!
Mr BROWNLOW:	Yes, I will. Oliver is different. He reminds me of someone – someone I can't recall. He'll be back.
	(Oliver is walking happily towards the bookstall when Nancy grabs hold of him.)
OLIVER:	*(Frightened)* Let go of me. *(Struggling)* Who are you? What do you want?
NANCY:	*(To the gathering crowd)* Oliver! Oliver! You naughty boy, to make me suffer such distress on your account. Thank heavens I've found you. My naughty brother, running away from your parents… making them break their old hearts.
1st BYSTANDER:	Young wretch!

2nd BYSTANDER: Go home to your mother, you little brute.

SCENE TWO

Oliver is crying in a corner of Fagin's room.

OLIVER: Mr Brownlow will think I stole the books. *(Tearful)* You have kidnapped me.

FAGIN: Ha, ha. So he will, so he will my dear.

OLIVER: *(Stands up and runs towards the door)* I have to get back, I don't want to live here with you, you're a thief!

NANCY: *(To Fagin)* We've done wrong, kidnapping the boy, Fagin.

BILL: *(Seeing Oliver trying to escape, calls his dog)* Bull's Eye, at him!

NANCY: *(Stepping between Oliver and the dog)* No, Bill. The dog will tear him to pieces.

FAGIN: *(Picking up a wooden club)* Then we'll knock some sense into the boy.

NANCY: No! You've got Oliver, what more would you have?

JACK: Don't hit him, Fagin. I'll teach him how to steal wipes.

BILL: *(Thinking)* I want a boy... a small, thin boy... for my housebreaking job. *(Points to Oliver)* He'll do... but train him first, *(Grabs Fagin's club)* and should he try to deceive us... I'll bash some sense into 'im.

(The following night, Fagin takes Oliver to Bill Sikes' house.)

FAGIN: *(Lighting a candle)* Oliver, *(Softly)* you may read until Sikes shows up.

OLIVER: Thank you, sir.

FAGIN: *(Softly)* Take heed, Oliver, take heed. Sikes is a rough man and thinks nothing of blood when he's in a bad mood. Whatever happens, say nothing and do as he bids you. I'd never have used the club against you, my dear… but Bill would and has used violence. Goodnight.

(Oliver starts to read a book, but falls asleep.)

NANCY: *(Entering the house)* Who's there?

OLIVER: Me, Oliver Twist. *(Nancy starts to cry then doubles up in despair)* Are you all right? Are you ill? Do you have a pain?

NANCY: *(Sobbing)* I never thought it would come to this.

OLIVER: What, Nancy?

NANCY: Oh, never mind. I don't know what comes over me, it's this place, my life. *(Pause)* I've come from Bill. *(Shudders)* He needs you.

OLIVER: To do harm?

NANCY: No *(laughs hysterically)* or yes. What does it matter? *(Shows Oliver her neck)* I gained these bruises to keep you from harm. Bill is a mean master. *(Kindly)* Now follow me, Oliver. If you don't hush, he'll beat you. *(They run along the streets, hand in hand)* This way, Oliver.

(They enter a house)

BILL: *(At the top of the stairs)* Come on!

(Oliver follows Bill Sikes. Nancy waves farewell to Oliver.)

I have a loaded gun, Oliver. Make a noise, say anything and I'll blow your brains out.

NANCY:	*(Re-enters the house and speaks to Oliver)* If you mess up this job, he'll shoot you and take his chances of swingin' for it afterwards.
BILL:	*(Overhearing)* That's it exactly!
	(Bill robs the house of silverware and Oliver places the items in a large sack)
	Tomorrow, the big one!
NARRATOR:	The following evening, Sikes takes Oliver to the outside of a large house.
BILL:	You have to squeeze through the pane, slip into the house, and unbolt the front door. Got it?
OLIVER:	No, sir. I'm not house-breaking or robbing.
BILL:	*(Nasty)* You'll do what I say or *(points pistol at Oliver's head)* I'll blow your brains out.
	(Oliver sneaks in at the window. There is a loud crash.)
	(Worried) Back, Oliver…back. They've heard us.

(Oliver runs to the window pane and tries to squeeze through. There is a sound of a shot.)

OLIVER: Oh, I'm hit.

BILL: *(To himself)* Blood everywhere. Damn! The boy bleeds!

(Oliver falls to the ground) That's him done for. Better get rid of the body… evidence!

SCENE THREE

NARRATOR: In the poorhouse, Sally is dying.

SALLY: *(To Mr Bumble)* She gave birth to a boy and died.

Mr BUMBLE: Yes, who did?

SALLY: *(Mumbling)* She wasn't even cold and I stole it.

Mr BUMBLE: Stole what, Sally?

SALLY: The only thing she had, poor soul. They'd have treated the child better if they'd known.

Mr BUMBLE: *(Confused)* Who? Treated who better?

SALLY: He growed so like his mother, poor sweet little boy.

Mr BUMBLE: The boy? What's his name?

SALLY: Oliver, they called him. I stole his mother's gold brooch. They called him Oliver... and on account of the gold brooch, I lied to Mr Monks. Oliver....that was...

(She dies)

Mr BUMBLE: Dear me, stone dead! And nothing to tell after all. But I know a Mr Monks. I'd better tell him all that has passed.

SCENE FOUR

Bill Sikes lays Oliver carefully down in a ditch. He hears men approaching from the house. They have dogs.

BILL: *(Shaking his fist at the men and the dogs)* Wolves tear your throats. I wish I was amongst some of you; you'd howl the hoarser for it! I'll drop the boy and run; or it'll be the gallows for me.

(Bill runs off)

BRITTLES: *(To his dogs)* Pitcher, Neptune, come here!

(To Giles) We ought to go home again.

GILES: You're afraid, Brittles.

BRITTLES: I ain't.

GILES: You are.

BRITTLES: You're a falsehood, Giles. *(Relenting)* It's natural and proper to be afraid, under such circumstances.

(Oliver struggles from the ditch, holding his bloody arm. He walks towards the men, as if in a dream.)

BRITTLES: *(Afraid)* What's that coming towards us?

GILES: A boy – must've been the one I shot.

BRITTLES: He'll hang for sure.

(Oliver faints)

GILES: *(lifting Oliver into his arms)* Let's get the lad to the house, before he dies.

(At the house, an old lady approaches the men.)

Mrs MAYLIE: What's the to-do?

GILES: We have an injured boy, ma'am.

MRS MAYLIE: Take him upstairs and fetch a doctor.

NARRATOR: Oliver stays with Mrs Maylie until, six months later, he has recovered. He is fit and in good health.

GILES: The missus has certainly taken a shine to you, Oliver.

OLIVER: I'm lucky.

BRITTLES: You certainly are lucky, Oliver lad. The old lady is rich, without relatives. Just play your cards right and you'll inherit a fortune. Better get on with your studies, Oliver. And don't forget the servants – even if we did shoot you.

(Oliver takes up a book and reads. Soon, he falls asleep. Fagin and the Artful Dodger sneak up to the window.)

FAGIN: *(To Jack)* Hush, my dear, it's him sure enough.

JACK: Come away, before he wakes up.

OLIVER: *(Waking up)* Fagin! *(Looks up)* He's gone. Was he a dream or reality?

NARRATOR: Meanwhile, Bill Sikes has fallen ill. He has been in bed for a week.

BILL: What time is it?

NANCY: Not long gone seven. How do you feel tonight, Bill?

BILL: As weak as water. Here, lend us a hand, and let me get off this thundering bed anyhow.

(Nancy walks away)

NANCY: You'd better be good to me tonight. I've nursed and cared for you as if you'd been a child. If it wasn't for me, you'd have died in your bed.

(Enter Fagin and the Artful Dodger)

BILL: I won't hit you tonight then. *(Sees Fagin)* What ill wind has blown you here, you old miser?

FAGIN: No ill wind at all, my dear. Evil winds blow nobody any good. I've brought you a bottle of gin.

(Bill grabs the bottle and drinks greedily. He pours his next drink into a tankard)

NANCY: *(pouring laudanum into Bill's next drink)* You wouldn't believe old Bill has been so ill.

FAGIN: *(Hands Bill money)* I have a job for you tonight.

BILL: *(Sits up in bed)* Ha, I feel better already. But *(yawn)* tired.

NANCY: You're still not well, Bill.

BILL: *(Sinking back on his bed)* Sleepy, so sleepy. *(Sits up for a moment)* Just a snooze, Nancy. Wake me for the burglary.*(Falls back on his bed)* Wake me later, Nancy.

(Bill falls asleep. Nancy ushers out Fagin and the Artful Dodger)

NANCY: *(To herself)* Now, I'll just have time to find Mrs Maylie.

SCENE FIVE

Nancy has arrived at Mrs Maylie's house. Mrs Maylie appears, leaning heavily on a stick.

Mrs MAYLIE: Well?

NANCY: *(Nervous)* I am about to put my life, and the lives of others, in your hands. *(Hesitates)* I am the girl who dragged young Oliver back to Fagin's house. I took him away from Mr Brownlow. *(She sobs)* Thank heavens Oliver has found good friends. All my life, the alley and the gutter were mine.

Mrs MAYLIE: You poor girl!

NANCY: I came to tell you that Fagin wants Oliver back.

Mrs MAYLIE: *(Indignant)* Well, he can't have Oliver!

NANCY: He wants Oliver dead. Oliver has an older half-brother, a man named Monks. Monks has struck a deal with Fagin.

Mrs MAYLIE: Well, I never did!

NANCY: Oliver is a good boy. *(Weeps)* I have risked my life for him. Meet me by London Bridge tomorrow night.

(Nancy runs off)

Mrs MAYLIE: Monks? I had better discover who this Monks is and why he wants to kill my little Oliver!

SCENE SIX

Mrs Maylie visits Mr Brownlow. Mr Grimwig is with Mr Brownlow.

MRS MAYLIE: Good afternoon, Mr Brownlow. I shall surprise you very much if I tell you that you once showed great kindness to a dear young friend of mine called Oliver Twist.

Mr GRIMWIG: A bad one. I'll eat my hat if he isn't a bad one.

Mrs MAYLIE: I have found Oliver to be a child of noble nature. He has a warm heart.

Mr BROWNLOW: Indeed! And you are?

Mrs MAYLIE: Mrs Maylie....you knew my husband.

Mr BROWNLOW: Maylie of Maylie Lodge?

MRS MAYLIE: Now I have a story to tell you that will make you feel kindly towards the boy.

NARRATOR: Mrs Maylie tells Mr Brownlow all that has happened to Oliver since he left Mr Brownlow's house, carrying the pile of books.

Mr BROWNLOW: Now, what shall we do?

Mr GRIMWIG: Hang the villains that kidnapped poor Oliver!

MRS MAYLIE: And the girl who informed on them?

Mr GRIMWIG: Transport her to the colonies.

MRS MAYLIE: We'll see her again, and I know how.

NARRATOR: That evening, Mr Brownlow and Mrs Maylie see Nancy walking up and down London Bridge. She is observed by the Artful Dodger and Noah Claypole who are hiding under the bridge.

Mrs MAYLIE:	*(Whispers)* Nancy?
NANCY:	Mrs Maylie? *(Nancy shudders)* I have a fear and dread on me tonight, I can hardly stand.
Mr BROWNLOW:	A fear of what?
NANCY:	*(Afraid)* Who are you?

Mr BROWNLOW:	A friend of Mrs Maylie. What do you fear, Nancy?
NANCY:	I do not know. I have horrible thoughts of death and I see shrouds with blood on them. A fear makes my heart burn as if I'm on fire. In a book I was reading, on every page was written the word coffin.
Mr BROWNLOW:	*(Strong)* Imagination!
NANCY:	*(Shudders)* No!

Mr BROWNLOW:	You are ready to deliver the villains up to the law?
NANCY:	Bad as they are, they never turned against me. I'll deliver up Monks, to save Oliver. I shall tell you all about his dirty dealings.

(Under the bridge)

JACK:	*(To Noah)* Glad you joined Fagin's gang, Noah?
NOAH:	*(Determined)* This is better than real work. If I can do work'us any disservice, I will!
JACK:	We'll tell Fagin all we've heard. This will be bad for Nancy.
NOAH:	I must get paid for this – to keep Charlotte, now we've run away from Mr Sowerberry's house.

(Nancy shakes Mr Brownlow's hand and she walks home. Jack and Noah run to Fagin's house. Later, Fagin is sitting counting his money. A box full of jewels lies open, next to him. There is a knock on the door. He hastily puts his box under the floorboards. He stuffs coins into his pockets. Bill Sikes, followed by his dog, enters the room.)

BILL:	Why did you send Artful Dodger round to my place? Why do you want to see me urgently? Don't you know I'm planning a job for tonight?
FAGIN:	*(Crafty)* What'd you do if someone was to peach on us, my dear? Supposin' someone was to blow on us, what'd you do?

(Bill stares at the sleeping figure of Noah Claypole.)

BILL: *(Pointing at Noah)* Him?

FAGIN: No, not him.

BILL: Whoever it was, I'd smash their brains out.

FAGIN: *(Quickly)* Nancy's blown on us.

BILL: *(Shocked)* Hell's fire!

FAGIN: *(Worried)* You won't be too violent on her,
Bill – I mean not too violent, for safety?

*(Bill smashes his fist into the wall. He looks at
his bleeding knuckles. He pushes Fagin onto the
floor and storms off to his own place. Nancy is
asleep. He shakes her, she looks at him and smiles.)*

NANCY: *(Half-asleep)* Bill's back, what a pleasure!

BILL: *(Roughly)* Is it? Get up!

(She does as she is told. He grabs her.)

NANCY: *(Afraid)* Bill, Bill! Tell me what I have done.

BILL: *(Angry)* You know, you she-devil! You've
peached on us.

NANCY: Not on us. Oh, you cannot have the heart to
kill me. Think of all I have done for you.
Don't spill my blood.

*(Bill picks up his pistol and fires. Nancy is struck
in the head. She falls, praying out to heaven. Bill,
in fury, hits her with his club.)*

BILL: *(To himself)* I've killed her. I'm a murderer!

(Bill throws down his club)

They'll know me because of my dog.

(He whistles for Bull's Eye, but the dog runs off)

Damn – it's as if the brute sensed I
was going to kill him.

SCENE SEVEN

Mr Brownlow is looking at the painting of a beautiful woman. The painting is hanging on the wall in his study.

Mr BROWNLOW: *(to himself)* I knew all along. I knew Oliver was her boy.

(Mr Monks enters. He has grown uglier and fatter than he was ten years ago.)

Mr MONKS: Why am I brought here?

Mr BROWNLOW: Because you are the oldest boy of my dead friend, Mr Leeford. You are Oliver's half-brother.

Mr MONKS: *(Defensive)* I have no brother. Why do you talk to me of brothers? I was an only child.

Mr BROWNLOW: *(Speaking quickly and with emotion)* My friend, your father separated from your mother – the woman he was forced to marry – when you were eleven. He fell in love with a beautiful girl – a naval officer's daughter. He would have married her, except he was called to Rome, urgently. There, he caught the fever and died. You and your mother inherited everything. Your father's girl had a child and died.

Mr MONKS: *(Shrugs)* Well, what of it?

Mr BROWNLOW: My friend, Mr Grimwig, has a will your father made before he journeyed to Rome. You and your brother share the inheritance.

Mr MONKS: Never! Prove it!

Mr BROWNLOW: I have a brooch with an inscription on it, found by Mr Bumble after an old lady died. The old lady took it from your father's girl when she herself died. I know you met old Sally, I know you have asked a man called Fagin to kill Oliver. I want you to give Oliver half your inheritance – or I shall see the police myself.

(Mr Grimwig bursts into the room)

Mr GRIMWIG: They are after the criminal, Sikes. His own dog is leading them to him. Fagin and the others are near capture.

Mr MONKS: *(Agitated)* I shall do all you say…and live abroad. I shall never trouble you again.

Mr BROWNLOW: Sign the documents Mr Grimwig has prepared and go!

(Mr Monks signs the documents. On his way out, he bumps into Mrs Maylie and Oliver.)

Mr MONKS: Out of my way!

Mrs MAYLIE: Excuse me, young man.

(She hits Mr Monks with her walking stick)

Now Oliver, tell Mr Brownlow what we have heard.

OLIVER: *(Sobs)* Nancy is dead. Horrible Bill Sikes murdered her.

(Oliver is overcome with emotion and he cries.)

Mrs MAYLIE:	But the police followed Sikes's dog. When they caught up with him, he climbed onto a roof to escape. He fell off the roof. *(snorts in disgust)* I expect he was full of drink. In short, he is dead.
OLIVER:	*(Tearful)* Fagin and the gang are arrested.

Mr BROWNLOW:	Splendid, Oliver, splendid. Now you are safe from the gang, and a rich young man, what would you like to do, Oliver?
OLIVER:	*(Wipes his eyes)* Live with you, Mr Brownlow. *(Hesitates)* If you meant what you once said – that I'd never be without a friend as long as you live.
Mr BROWNLOW:	Oliver, my home is your home.
Mrs MAYLIE:	And you can visit me as often as you like.
Mr BROWNLOW:	I shall introduce you to people of your own age, too. You deserve a good life after all your troubles, Oliver!
OLIVER:	Thank you, Mr Brownlow.

OLIVER TWIST

ACTIVITIES
ACT ONE: SCENES ONE TO FOUR

Improvisation
In groups, imagine you are the boys in the workhouse. You are plotting against Oliver, to make sure he receives the short straw. Henry and Ben are in the play, but there would be others in the group. Discuss your plans amongst yourselves and make sure Oliver is the one to ask for more food.

Hot-seating
Try to remember as many facts as possible. In groups of three or four, hot-seat the following characters from scene four:

Mr Sowerberry - he might be able to piece together what happened from Oliver, Mrs Sowerberry, and Noah Claypole. Why does he fail to believe Oliver? Or is he afraid to go against his wife?

Mrs Sowerberry - what does she think about Oliver and why does she believe Noah's version of events?

Noah -why is he so horrible to Oliver? Why is he willing to allow Oliver to be so cruelly punished? How does he feel after Oliver hits him?

Oliver - he has never seen his mother, so why is he so upset? Why has he decided to run away and what are his plans for the future?

Writing
In pairs, find out as much as possible about Mr Bumble. Re-read the scenes involving Mr Bumble. What do the scenes tell us about Mr Bumble's character and appearance? Write all you know about him.

You are Oliver. Write about your life so far. You will need to mention your time at the workhouse and your time with the Sowerberrys. Say why you felt the need to run away.

ACT ONE: SCENE FIVE

Discussion
In Dickens' original novel, we are meant to dislike Fagin. He was Jewish and there is a great deal of anti-semitism in pre-twentieth century English literature. Go through scene five and list all the disagreeable things about Fagin.

Improvisation
Oliver is caught by Mr Brownlow. Although he has done no wrong, Oliver is accused of stealing. Improvise the scene when Jack takes the handkerchief, and Mr Brownlow believes Oliver is the thief.

Improvise the scene between Mr Fang, Mr Brownlow and Oliver. How long did they wait for Mr Fang, the magistrate? What was spoken between the policeman, Mr Brownlow and Oliver before Mr Fang arrived?

Writing
Look at some of the characters in this scene. What are they like? Copy out and complete the list.

Character	Points to Notice	Evidence
Mr Fang	Rude	Pretended Mr Brownlow was the accused.
Mr Brownlow		
Bill		
Nancy		

Imagine Fagin and the gang are listening to Jack. He is telling them how Oliver was caught and what will happen to him. They want Oliver back, or he may 'peach' on them. They discuss plans. Write notes, and add an extra scene into this play. The first few lines have been done for you.

Extra scene

Jack: Hello all.

Fagin: *(rubbing his hands together)* Any wipes, Jack?

Jack: Yeah!

Nancy: What's happened to the boy, Jack?

Jack: *(hesitates)* Boy? What boy?

Nancy: Don't give us that, the little boy, Oliver!

(Now continue the scene)

ACT TWO: SCENES ONE AND TWO.

Discussion
Mr Grimwig (scene one) warns Mr Brownlow about Oliver. Is he right to do so? After all, Oliver came from the workhouse and was seen with a criminal (Jack). Should he trust and help a boy he does not know?

What do we learn about Bill in these scenes?

Mr Bumble (scene three) knows that Oliver's mother had a gold brooch. Why does he decide to tell Mr Monks? What else could he have done? How does this scene change our view of Mr Bumble?

Writing
Mr Brownlow is keeping a diary. What might he write about Oliver's disappearance?

ACT TWO: SCENES FOUR TO SEVEN.

Discussion
What do you feel about Bill as the play progresses? Do you feel any pity for him? Explain your feelings, using evidence from the text.

Freeze-framing
Freeze from the moment that Bill lays Oliver in the ditch. Brittles and Giles could be in the distance. Think of all that has taken place and what facial expressions and positions each person might have.

Hot -seating
Bill - after he has killed Nancy. Why did he kill her, does he regret her death?

Noah - after he hears about Nancy's death. How does he feel about 'peaching' on Nancy? Did he expect Bill to be violent?

Fagin - does he regret telling Bill all that Noah told him? How did he expect events to turn out? Has he any regrets about running a gang of criminals?